Galaxies and the Gulf of Virtual In

CW01338125

PROLOGUE – Talia Enter the Mea

I am a boy. My name is Talia, and I am ill-equipped for the meatgrinder of life.

Everything is confusing. Each day is difficult, and brings labours that would seem simple to others.

If I'm late leaving the house for work, it's raining. If I take the bus to work, there's a hole in my pocket. If there's cash in my other pocket, the bus turns out to be the wrong one.

If I eventually get to work, I don't fit into the regime of programmable automatons that talk quietly, but enthusiastically about television and sport. If I'm working, the factory is suddenly underwater, the boxes and crates encrusted with the aggressively armoured shells of tiny crustaceans, the ocean filled with threat, and my shoes are slippery.

If I'm collecting corn, there are only toadstools, most of which are headless and the stumps blackened. I stand tall and erect in a sea of stumps. There are coins among the crops, but they cannot belong to me. My jubilation would betray me, and I'd become as prey. With my basket of ailing fungi, I am suddenly naked, and in my pursuit of shelter it snows, my progress hampered by brutal winds. The roads are ice, tearing at the flesh of my bare feet. Balloons are attached to my fingers, their short strings tight and irritating. They thrash against my head and face, teasing me, mocking me, and then they blow away.

The weather is always treacherous.

I want to stand on the shoulders of giants. Conversely, I enter the meatgrinder. I am smashed beneath the skulls of the aborted babies.

ACT 1 – Chaten's Lute

In the dead world of Chaten's Lute, the once proud and all-conquering human race lived like worms in a festering corpse. Although still the dominant species, they numbered few, inhabiting crumbling cities and adhering to no governing body. Wind whistled and rain fell upon streets that stood defiant against the decay. Precious few houses could assume the title of dwelling.

One such house was sealed against the elements. Its windows were boarded with crooked, mould-spotted timbers, its contents precious. Inside the dilapidated building two people sheltered, a boy and an infant. Both sat on the smooth, dry dirt of the ground floor, the floorboards having been scavenged in some distant, prior chapter. Leaning against one wall, they chatted amiably, despite the apparent age differential.

"So why do you feel you've got to go?" asked the infant. "What is it that drives you?"

"Cor blimey, I don't know," replied the boy. "This just doesn't seem real to me."

"Yes," the boy reluctantly admitted. "That certainly felt real." He replaced his cloth.

The infant inscribed an unremarkable design into the dirt floor with one chubby finger. "Define real," she implored. "After all, I am ancient. Here I sit in the body of a child, and yet once I was the wife of Lot. Explain that!"

"I can't," he said. "Suffice it to say that you are the 'Morph. It's your choice that you assume the infant's guise."

The 'Morph looked up thoughtfully. "Wouldn't it be amusing, if this house were upside-down? The floor being the ceiling, the ceiling being the floor. Wouldn't you like that?"

"For a short time probably," said the boy. "You'd have to keep stepping over that section of wall above the doorways. And the light fitting would lie uselessly upon the floor."

"Uselessly? Oh I think it would be fun! Something that's fun should not be useless."

The boy turned away, dreaming of life in a city that still thrived, a high street along which people bustled and were parted from their monies. In his reminiscence, traffic crawled through congested roads that criss-crossed the city, contaminating the air. In front of him, close enough to touch, walked the 'Morph, now assuming the form of a young woman; although there was little to suggest that this youth *was* the his baby companion, he simply knew it was so. Her hair was quite short, tousled. She was slender and attractive.

"I've got no tits," she announced, turning momentarily to meet his gaze. "You'll find that out later." She smirked tantalisingly, her eyes like polished sapphires.

At that moment, the boy's heart swelled with a surprising love for the 'Morph, and right then he knew he would die for her. A tear threatened to bloom in the corner of one eye as he relished the sweet anticipation of what she promised. He pictured her small breasts, nipples like pink bullets. He imagined massaging them, leaning over her naked body, his hands longing for a more plentiful bounty, yet at the same time knowing that they would never hold a more precious cargo.

"No! I knew you'd bungle it!" the pretty 'Morph complained, her eyes flooded with disappointment. "You're clumsy, an oaf!" She pushed his desperate, grasping hands away from her flesh.

A sharp intake of breath, and the boy returned his attention to the infant, who sat innocently examining the tip of one finger that was coated with dust. Behind her on the wall there hung a horseshoe arrangement of silver-shelled beetles, their wing cases shining like mirror-glass. The unusual congregation of beetles quickly drew his undivided attention, their sudden appearance as vivid and disturbing as a narcotic flashback. The clicking of their naturally armoured legs, multiplied into a chirruping chorus of tiny voices bothered him like the accidental shriek of a fork on a ceramic plate.

"They're not real," the 'Morph muttered, sounding bored.

The boy turned to look at her, momentarily distracted. "Hm?" he enquired.

"The silver coins," she said, now irritated.

"W-what coins?" he asked. When he looked for the beetles again, they had vanished.

Sighing, he settled back against the wall, its dry, flaky surface now irritatingly cool against his bare flesh. Within moments, however, his blood had warmed it, and it became comfortable.

"You're scared I'll leave aren't you?" he asked of the baby.

"I shouldn't like to admit that I'm scared, exactly," she said.

"Then why the elaborate theatrics?"

"Theatrics?" she repeated, suddenly vexed. "A child throwing a tantrum may make great use of theatrics!"

"A child you are," he goaded. "A baby." He turned away again.

After a short time, a scent came to him, subtle, yet wholly intoxicating. Reluctant to face what he was convinced would be further subterfuge, he continued to gaze somewhere beyond the exterior wall he was facing. The scent, however, was too alluring; had he been sealed in a tiny cell of warm garbage for time beyond endurance, then released upon a beach to refresh his respiratory system with the crisp, clear air of the surf, he could not have been more appreciative of its balm. His head swam, flooded with soothing sensibilities, sensations of nurture that finally danced across his scalp like ants. Powerless to resist, he turned to face the source of the fragrance, wanting, *needing* to drink of its sweet, floral bouquet. There stood the 'Morph.

A grown woman, to call her beautiful would have been woefully inadequate. Blonde hair fell from her head like liquid gold in which the dab of a divine hand had caused concentric ripples to swell throughout. Her face, fine featured, and yet not severely so, was sufficient to send the boy's mouth agape and spill tears of bliss from his stricken eyes into the dirt. Her lips, exquisite and cherry-red, were as sharp-edged as a crescent moon against the cloudless night sky. He dared not even long to kiss them, merely to behold was privilege enough; to touch, he felt, would be trespass. Eyes of brilliance and dark wonders, boundless knowledge and innocence indivisible observed him as he fed upon ambrosia. Below her neck was a sculpted body, pearl pale and fashionably attired; fashionably, that is, for the most closely relevant civilised period. Jaw slack, he stared in awe.

"What's your name?" he whispered, afraid that his voice, given strength, would be sufficient to shatter this delicate jewel.

"You've always known it," she replied, her voice buoyant, musical.

"You won't stay, will you?" he asked, fearful of a negative response and yet concurrently joyful that he had known these moments with this facet of the 'Morph.

"No," she answered softly, her mouth bending to smile, lending warmth to her sorrowful eyes.

As her eyes stared into his, her hair lost its subtle waves, yet none of its appeal. It grew straight as corn stalks, each strand glistening with natural luminescence. The boy dared to touch it. It slithered across his fingers, as fine as spider-silk.

"Where are you going?" he asked.

"Away," she said quietly, still smiling.

Unable to refrain, he leaned forward and kissed the 'Morph's latest embodiment. Her lips, soft and pliant, met his willingly, and responded to his ardour. He tasted of her breath, like a sweet aphrodisiac, then drew back to look upon her once more, lest she be gone.

Once more their eyes locked and everything around them disappeared within a wash of brilliant light, like Winter sun reflected on a window. He drew her close to him, his arms tightly enfolding her. He closed his eyes, branding the experience of these past few moments into his memory with what he hoped would be the utmost clarity; still he breathed deeply of her perfume. Then his arms held nothing but air, and she was gone.

Reluctant to return to the cruel reality that was the sealed house in Chaten's Lute, the boy let his arms fall by his sides, his eyes yet closed, clinging to his precious memory.

"What *are* you doing?" asked the baby, her unmistakable voice dispelling his illusion like a reflection on water sullied by a thrown stone.

He sighed deeply, a further measure of his lust for life spewing from his lungs like fatted flies rising from the stinking remains of a dead animal. "I'm wishing I 'ad some bullets. Silver preferably."

"What on earth do you want bullets for?" she enquired.

"I should like to shoot a wolf," he replied.

"I'm sure I've no idea what you're talking about," the 'Morph went on. "How would a wolf get in here? And besides that, you don't own a gun."

"No," he said.

He opened his eyes and was rewarded with the drab vista of damp grey plaster and dust. Against one wall rested the infant, unmoved and unchanged. Anger flared within him, then dissipated like so many fantastical dreams from a waking mind. What could he do? Violence was unthinkable, and ultimately pointless.

Shoulders slumped dejectedly, he made his way across the room to the infant, who looked up at him with such blatant admiration that he could not help but think it feigned. He lowered himself to the floor, once more assuming his place next to her. Like before, the flesh of his narrow back was assaulted upon contact with the wall, cold as a corpse. As before, his blood quickly warmed it and he began worrying at the frayed edges of his loincloth with fingers he could not still.

"You obviously intend us to remain here until we die," he stated.

"Good grief," began the 'Morph. "Here I am in an advanced embryonic state…and you speak of death!"

"Why do you insist that we remain within this *dismal* building?" he asked, unable to mask his building anger and frustration.

"I have no power over your right to a decision," she said curtly. "If you wish to leave, then peel back the boards and abandon me."

"Where would I go?" he warbled. "How far would my feet carry me before a little voice called to me on the breeze? You have an iron leash about my neck and each day you test it! And do you know what's most infuriating? What's most infuriating is that each day you deny these sly yanks of my chain!"

"I deny them and rightly so. Sometimes I think you spend too much time gazing at the moon."

"Sometimes I wish I was *on* the bloody moon!" he added. "Or that you were!"

The infant began to cry. Not the snuffling, shoulder-heaving sobs of a lady mourning, but the feeding cry of a genuine man-child. Listlessly the boy reached across and gathered her in his arms, a series of deft movements that spoke of routine. As he did so, her lips began to smack greedily, like the mouths of bottom-feeding fish. He raised her eager lips to his nipple, and at once she began to suckle, her flawless cheeks pulsing as if in the action of conveying milk, which of course, was nonsense.

ACT 2 – The Hum, the Phenomenon

If one should take a moment, late at night, when the world is as close to silent as this purportedly civilised world can get, it is possible to hear the hum. Anyone *can* hear it, but not everyone *will* hear it. As a general, but perhaps discomforting rule, the vast and idiosyncratic majority have to be made aware of something in order to appreciate it. As with a mild case of tinnitus, most will tune out the hum, or maybe dismiss it as a distant industrial discharge. But it is not.

The hum is a phenomenon. A myth made real. Nothing quite so wholesome as a tooth fairy, but with a great deal more substance. The hum will hum. It will hum at night, in its comfortable darkness. Prior to a traffic accident, there will typically be a squeal of tyres on tarmac; prior to a cinematic shark attack, a cello concerto. Lions roar, kestrels cry. The hum will hum.

Is the hum dangerous? Not the hum; the sound, but the hum; the phenomenon is made from fear of the unknown. It is borne of wounding and pain, its cells a weave of misery and malice. Conceived in the bleakest moments of war, baptised to the exquisite lament of a most desperate moment, the hum; the phenomenon is the wretched mongrel offspring of every wilfully broken promise. Its mandibles are the nails with which Jesus was crucified. Through ignorance, man made it so.

So as the boy with his faux-infant companion lay down to sleep in the ravaged world of Chaten's Lute, long after worldwide social collapse, beyond the extinction of motorcars and commerce, so did the fanciful wanderings of his mind eventually draw his attention to the hum.

"Can you hear that?" he asked of the infant.

"All I hear is your heart," she replied. "Like a drum to scare the boggarts from my bedside."

The boy sighed, deeply and despondently. He settled his head upon a pillow stuffed with manually manipulated paper, but he could not avert his attention from the hum.

"Something's 'umming," he announced. "Sounds like bees. *Billions* of bees."

"I could foretell your reaction to a billion bees. You were dumbstruck with fear when you saw that gnu dying."

"That wasn't a gnu, it was something between a pelican and a flamingo. What's more, it was a monster! It could've stomped an 'ole right through me!"

"Please cease your rattling," the infant whined. "I'm so tired I could just die."

The boy obeyed, in as far as his rattling concluded, because to flout the 'Morph's wishes meant typically incurring some form of elaborate mind control which usually left him feeling used and somewhat flogged. He would wait until the infant slumbered, then investigate the hum; the sound. It worried at him like a tiny foreign body such as gravel inside the manufactured shoes he used to wear.

As the shadows deepened in the room the unlikely team shared, as the hum; the phenomenon scratched its way around the perimeter of the house like an ant on a wrapped sweet, the boy watched the slow, regular pulse of the infant's respiration.

Unperceived (he perceived), he sneakily hefted himself from the bed and onto the tamped dirt of the floor. Making his way through the shadows to the one boarded-up window through which he knew from familiarity a meagre draught blew, he found he could only discern the hum; the sound when he was completely static. Like one incarcerated, he laid a hand against the boards, feeling the whisper of freedom blow tantalisingly across his fingers. He married his face to his hand, relishing even the cold dampness of the coloured dots of mould that adorned the timbers; garish and soothing. The slivers of wind lapped at his eyes, bringing to both a fresh and pure tear to sip. Gently at first, but then with a force of one become legion, he pushed at the aged wood.

It didn't splinter, that damp, rotted wood, so much as it *sighed* free of the nails that pinned it to its stouter cousins. It bumped onto the tarmac outside, an obsolete road riven by unchecked flora. The boy was assailed by wind and rain. Recoiling, he avoided contact with what appeared to be a stunted, tailless rat borne upon the legs of a spider crab, as it slid through the slotted window like the first drop of blood from a stiletto murder.

The gravity of his actions fell upon him like a weighted net. He had created an aperture; a window to the savage *outside*, an open wound to infection. Should he desire it, escape was possible. Conversely, he had introduced a bad cell to the malodorous animal that he and the infant occupied like parasitic partners.

As if on cue, she spoke from somewhere that sounded like the outskirts of a dream, "Time is a healer, but also a stealer. In the morning you'll care less, but you'll have less time to care."

He looked to the dirt at his feet, hanging his head in exasperation and guilt. Between his feet, bold and surreal, was approximately a tablespoonful of cooked rice. Like healthy teeth in a dead gum, the grains of rice glowed; not with brilliance, exactly, but with promise. As he watched, they blurred, the edges furring as if his vision was marred by tears.

He blinked repeatedly, and looked up as the walls around him fell away into white light like dereliction into the curl of a tornado. As the walls fell away, so his anxieties abated. As they did, so grew an almost tangible, inexplicable emotional bond for the handful of uniformed men that now surrounded him. From the inside of the light they had come. They had saved him, he felt. They had carried him, and now they strode at his side, faces determined and each step sure. Brothers in arms; a unit forged in undisclosed adversity via an indistinct adversary.

"We did it," said the nearest soldier, in a quaking voice that didn't quite fit. "We're safe now. The war is over for us."

The boy was befuddled. He marched alongside the vocal soldier as if drugged. Following blind compulsion, he walked a landscape stricken by conflict. All about them lay ruins of civilisation; twisted, devastated buildings, with scarcely more than litter and ashes occupying what were once streets. The soldier was grinning broadly, a smile that didn't touch his eyes; eyes that were cold, desperate and terminal.

"When someone you love dies," the soldier went on, his pitch erratic like static. "They will visit you in a dream. You may not understand the message, but they will touch you all the same."

The soldier's manic countenance fixed upon him. "You're dead, soldier," he concluded.

The cries of the infant brought him back; the feigned cries of a mimic.

The rat-crab thing was loose in the house.

“A boggart!” screamed the infant. “You willingly brought a boggart!”

“Where is it?” he asked, dazed; temporarily dismissing all queries and doubts of the world-war-period episode and its origins.

“Where is what?” she snapped. “The Fluv? The Fluv was the revolutionary games console of the future, and now it’s jettisoned.”

“Your boggart,” he answered with little conviction. “I have an idea what might’ve ‘appened to your boggart.”

He turned to the crudely boarded window, which held fast as it always had, at least during the current occupation. Neither wind nor rain, nor harbinger of death had entered.

The boy slumped, landing clumsily, sitting cross-legged in the dirt.

Moments later the infant asked “Was it your grandfather in the dream?”

“No,” he answered. “It was whichever *pawn* you put there to tease me.”

“Not just now,” she scolded. “The other night. When you wept in your sleep.”

“Yes. I think so, although it didn’t look like him. ‘Least, not as I remember him. Was *that* your doing too?”

“Was *what* my doing?”

“Is it now that even my dreams aren’t sacred?”

“Nothing is sacred,” hissed the infant. She whispered like winter wind through the weave of a canopy of frozen branches above seemingly endless frozen graves, each one marking a decaying shell of a life that once was, and now reeked. Her breath plumed from her tiny, exquisite lips as she spoke. "All there is to rape," she went on. "Everything is bounty to be touched and soiled, broken and mourned."

The boys head swam to the music of her words, his brain writhing in the oxymoron of an ecstatic lament. His eyes rolled backward in his head, his mouth agape.

"Your clowns and fairies await butchery," she said, each word forming in a mouth that spoke with a most archaic, learned sincerity. Every syllable fell like an elaborate shard of ice detaching from a seemingly infinite web of translucent complexity, tumbling to strike others, creating a fading cascade of deific music. "As do the children they were conceived to amuse. Your world was a painted smile of blood. Each time the sun rose, the blackness below stairs grew denser as angels were trussed and gutted. Given light and life, you created boundaries and bullets. It strangles and it kills. What fate was theirs; is yours."

From behind the boy came a growling; a primitive and loveless sound. He turned to see a black hound, visibly rabid, infected. Its baleful eyes fixed on him, and he fled for the stairs, certain that he hadn't the time to climb them before the dog would catch him and visit its sweating, primal brand of suffering upon him. Driven by survival instinct he powered up the skeletal staircase, heedless of protruding nails and splinters, the dog's hellacious cacophony so close at his heels he could *feel* the sound bouncing around the cavities of his ear canals. He reached the landing and looked around, lacking familiarity. Rain fell in the upper level; a gentle, peaceful rain. The hound had gone.

About him lay disorder; dust and books, pebbles and nails. Scarred were the white-painted beams that held this area together. Crumbling were the ceilings, and crooked were the doors; let the audience applaud you, for they'll overlook your flaws. The boy was not alone, he felt. Although the hound had vanished, he sensed a new threat lurking, and by and by, something rasped among the flotsam. Wood began to creak protestingly, and two diminutive humanoids emerged, mischievous urchins dressed in garish, soft fabrics in the style of *before-the-great-fall.* Their sneaking, prowling mannerisms hinted that their intentions were most dishonourable. They beheld an unnatural aura that sang of something that didn't belong, a misplaced surrealism he must instinctively defend against, crushing to dust at all cost.

With the arrival of the whelps, the room appeared to shift, elongating like warm toffee. The rear wall receded almost to a vanishing point, and the piles of detritus assembled themselves into scenic wings in the style of renaissance theatre. The stage set, the closest intruder made a scampering advance, and the boy planted his foot squarely in its chest, hoping to knock his would-be assailant to the floor. Instead, he was rewarded with an explosion; a cloud of stinking flies, swirling and seething around one another in a fractal-like fashion which could have been entrancing, had he not been labouring in a state of panic. The whole situation reeked of subterfuge. He seized the remaining whelp about the collar, and wrestled it to the floor, grinding its face upon the boards until its pathetic struggles ceased. Its serrated metal teeth snagged the flaking timbers, and all was still, save for the fine rain which had fallen throughout.

He pondered as he stared listlessly at the row of uniform teeth, whence these creatures had come. The jagged incisors held fast to the floor, their edges keen and perhaps suited to this final purpose. Beneath his hand, within the dome of the urchins head, there was almost certainly a brain. Within the brain, maybe there were ideas and dreams, incarcerated now and forever, dormant in the confines of the fabricated skull. The skull was riveted to the strip of metal that bristled with the urchins teeth, and the juvenile teeth bound the unit to the earth.

The broken-bone cleaning zone is closed for business, go on home.

Roll your own bones where *you* care to roam.

This old home is showing its foam. Set down and keep on burnishing that chrome.

'fore that gets tarnished too.

ACT 3 – Like Vinegar

Douglas stood in the grand foyer in a state of great excitement and nervous anticipation. In the typical style of such venues, the lavish area was a resplendent layout of plush carpets, gaudy polished railings and neon accessories. A fitting backdrop to the rock and roll star of recent times that our man was waiting to meet. Since adolescence he'd followed the star's career, rarely faltering. Now, having crossed the metaphorical bridge spanning the waters that marked the boundary of his better years, he finally had the opportunity to meet his idol one to one.

The wait was over. Here came the celebrity that had fronted one of the biggest rock and roll outfits of our time, who had performed acts of great athleticism on and off the stage, wowing audiences for decades, and, of course, selling countless thousands of records.

Douglas (affectionately Dougy) wasn't disappointed by the somewhat diminutive gentleman that approached him, flanked by token attendants, but found it difficult to suppress his astonishment at the rock star's obvious physical decline. He was still in awe of the singer's powerful presence and remarkable history, and so embraced him and rather ostentatiously, kissed his face. The rock legend ran through a series of perfunctory actions, his flamboyance *almost* masking the mechanical bent of his idiosyncrasies. Not so easily disguised were the deep lines marring his famous face, the thin lifelessness of his once-spectacular mane, or the tremor of his arthritic hands. Douglas, however, wasn't derailed. This, for him, had been a milestone event he would never forget. For hours following the meeting, a lyric from one of the band's more prominent hit singles echoed in his mind. "*Someone was with me that night as I lay again with the truth.*"

-O-

In a dusty, sandy wasteland, elsewhere in time, on a neglected edge of the new world, there stood the seemingly self-proclaimed Museum of Natural Horrors, and business was slow. Nestled within a horseshoe arrangement of dilapidated buildings stood a long-abandoned clutch of petrol pumps. Tied around one of the pumps with wire was a hand-painted billboard blowing and bumping in the incessant wind; it announced the aforementioned MUSEUM OF NATURAL HORRORS. The billboard was accurate, in that it was surrounded by natural horrors of varying age and quality. Less than two feet from the sign lay the dessicated body of a man, still sporting most of a voluminous Afro-Caribbean hairstyle. He was pointing to something over his head, a gesture that, like so many things in the civilised world which had once held such import, was lost.

"But I don't know if it matters," came a juvenile, feminine voice somewhere close by.

Unmoved by this apparent dismissal of his final act, the afro-man continued to languish in the sun, his eye sockets filled with stirring sand. Around him were similar corpses, some little more than skeletons, but all assailed by the desert, and no longer of any interest to flies.

Behind the former petrol station forecourt was a public convenience, a rather extravagant block where previously, a person/persons could make toilet or even take a shower. Long dry was the shower block, as were the cisterns, although the ammoniac aroma of stale urine remained.

"Outside, an apocalyptic storm was always raging." The voice again, echoed by the myriad tiles, simultaneously dampened by the errant sand.

It was an infant, the source of the voice, but only in guise. In truth it was an ancient being, blessed of a great many supernatural abilities, including the power to change form. The baby mask, however, more than suited her needs for the most part. Beside her sat a boy, sinewy, agile and scantily clad. The boy rested atop a crudely fashioned backpack, their limited necessities slung together and trussed up with makeshift twine. The museum of natural horrors made an ideal temporary shelter against the punishing, swirling sand, but a home it was not. The ablutions block was safe enough by day, but at night the dresdens gained substance. Sinister creatures were the dresdens, and responsible for most of the corpses strewn about the forecourt. Beneath the glare of the sun, only their footsteps were traceable in the sand, and they were harmlessly intangible. But at the setting of the sun their furry forms became visible, dwarven in stature, their only discernible facial features being the concave suggestion of eyes. Their latent motive, seemingly, was to silently kill.

"It's not a spider, it's an angel," said the baby.

The boy stirred from his rest, reluctantly opening his sandblasted eyes. "Who?!" he asked.

"I did already explain," she admonished. "I don't know if it matters!"

"It's 'ard to follow you from one moment to the next," said the boy, in his East-London-chestnut-seller brogue.

"Honestly, sometimes you have all the practical worth of pork paper!" she said, exasperated.

"Pork paper?" inquired the boy.

"A dietary staple, popular in the old ways."

"Shouldn't we get moving," the boy grudgingly suggested.

The baby sighed. "Yes, for fear of the dresdens."

She crawled into the jumble of the backpack, at once lending it her weight, and lending weight to the illusion that the boy travelled alone. He hefted the bundle about his shoulders and made his way out onto the sand. As they travelled, and as sunlight diminished, their shadows lengthened and the desolate dresdens descended on their wake, finding only empty tracks and trace evidence. A dresden was a hollow existence, stimulated, and sustained by sensory perception, particularly that of suffering. They relished the residual scent of the now-departed couple, and marvelled at the fresh, warm shapes they had left on the sand, yet mourned for the exquisite taste of their pain, and to feel their throes of hapless panic, for the opportunity was now lost.

In truth, even collectively, the 'Morph would have smote them.

Her distant voice reached the dresdens' sensitive ears, carried far on the still night air. She sang "Within the circle that aged, but wasn't ageing, all were sinners and the fat got fatter. Someone soothed me with soft, rhythmic gestures of love, but I don't know if it matters."

-O-

Floating in a retrospective joy following his illuminating evening, Douglas made his way home through the quiet, winding avenues of his home town. The street lamps offered a comforting, ambient glow that coupled with the subtle clicking of his boots on the tarmac to induce a feeling of general contentment in his already elated mind. What further toils in life had he, now that he'd faced his god? What further wonders could his remaining years present?

As he approached the long, familiar block of terraced houses that ran parallel to the street where he lived, he became aware of an irregular movement at one of the boarded-up ground floor windows of the Gailey house; strange for a house which had stood empty for as long as he could remember. Cautiously, he continued toward the gable end, and watched as the painted yellow board covering the window bulged rhythmically under a persistent barrage of apparent blows from within. The moist wood suddenly split with a delicious racket, halting Douglas in his tracks and revealing a sliver of flickering light suggestive of a fire. Still, the blows continued.

"Can I help?" Douglas offered, alarmed and shaken.

Through the fissure there came a cry, an amalgamation of pain and rage. Dirt-caked fingers forced the aperture wider, superseded by a flood of sylphid, spider-like creatures, their legs flexible like hair. *Angels,* thought Douglas absently. He recoiled, but not before a quantity of the bizarre arachnids had alighted on the bare flesh of his arm, borne upon the breeze like dandelion seeds. As he tried to brush them away, a cloud blew from beyond the split board, a billow of dust, spiders and threadlike worms. The cloud fell about him, the pests adhering to his skin. Where there were no means of entry into Douglas' body, they bit and made their own. He stood, frozen in a maelstrom of fear, repulsion and disbelief as the boards were rent apart and the bleeding, malformed occupants dragged him inside.

He lay upon the bare boards and dirt of the Gailey house, his captors having relinquished their grip. The pests, and the germ they carried, now ravaged his system, infecting him and implementing terrible and irreversible metamorphosis. Soon, all that had been Douglas was but a fading light, and the usurper had complete control. Fury and spite now empowered the changeling thing that got slowly to its feet, its skin splitting in places under the tension of the growth and deformities that were occurring. It slouched under the new mass of its left arm, the bones having elongated, the muscles undergoing incredible development, the skin toughening and mottling into a hard, chitinous exoskeleton. The animal, formerly Douglas, raised its huge, club-like arm and bellowed a cry that spoke of a fresh allegiance and primal appetite for dominion. The thread-worms and spiders now swarmed upon the twisted form of what had become an animal warhammer for causes as yet unknown.

Fires spat and crackled harmlessly around the ruin of the Gailey ground floor, casting dancing shadows around the rooms, silhouetting the vaguely humanoid figures that had dragged formerly-Douglas into this hell. The new warhammer approached the wall that joined the Gailey house to its neighbour and began to pound. Angry, panicked voices came from beyond the brick and plaster that crumbled under the onslaught of the giant arm, giving way to reveal light and warmth, which in turn, would give way to further desolation, chaos and loathing. Thread-worms floated on the updraughts of the new house, seeking fresh hosts, as did the angel-spiders that crawled obscenely into the virgin environment. The warhammer eventually strode through the riven dividing wall, followed by his new cohorts in their tooth and claw pursuit of the same sudden and cruel recruitment procedure they'd inflicted upon him. Great steaming tendrils of saliva depended from his shovel mouth as he swung his abnormally misshapen head in search of further conquest. Whatever the origins of this infestation, who quells the malefaction and disintegration? Whatever the motivation of this tyranny and degradation, can we, in ablution, regain our station? The warped and tiny, single-function brain of the warhammer cared not for such trivialities. Indefatigably, it moved on to the next dividing wall; the next conveniently-packed batch of pitiably protesting specimens, and the next cell to be infected.

Wall after wall fell, and home after home was breached under the advance of the ever-increasing army. Eventually, the din of destruction and the flames of malcontent caught the attention of those outside of the tormented containment. Authorities were contacted, and small crowds accrued. They chattered nervously, speculating with regards to the antagonists. Ronald, (affectionately Ronnie) a local self-professed organiser of men and all-round good egg stepped forward and assumed the role of leader and spokesperson. Ronnie enthused the congregation to step back from what was obviously a hazardous situation, and await instruction from emergency services. His advice was heeded, to some degree, and with limited success, as a great explosion of bricks and cement preceded the wailing sirens of the police. Amid the dust and smoke surrounding the cavity that been blown outward from the final house in the terrace, stood the warhammer. Audaciously, he/it surveyed the gathered flock.

His hands outstretched, palms foreward in a show of peace, Ronnie stammered "W-w-what...?"

Already, thread-worms and angel-spiders had begun to infect the crowd of bewildered onlookers, silently and undetected. Unrepentant, the warhammer turned his head up to the sky and spewed a further mist of said parasites into the night air. The wind took the mist as its own, and great the storm became.

Who shall inherit the earth, but an enemy that can scarce be fought? Who falls quicker than an army that was bought? What spoils await the victor if he gains only soured ground? And when there are no spoils left to reap, who exists to hold the vanquisher in renown?

"I don't know if it matters," the baby continued, far away, and the crowd began to fight among themselves.

ACT 4 – Tin Edge

And so a seed fell from space, and the seed was nourished, because here on earth our soils were rich.

We built a government, then joined hands against unity, running blindly into flames.

Though flesh was seared and rent, and mouths gape, filled with the remains of years, we shall lament.

Always our fate, to ululate.

The baby studied the brilliant glowing orb with a sullen expression. Grim were its contents, because they showed only doom. She turned her head this way and that, searching for what seemed a most elusive hope, but still death stared keenly back. The boy's clumsy antics, stumbling and scraping, brought her back to the present and she dismissed the vessel.

"Why the cacophony?" she asked, galled.

The boy flinched at her voice, so intent he'd been at his task of ridding the hollow of fat, black salamanders and the potential threat they posed. He thrust at the last remaining pest with his long pole, which bent under the stress of the poisonous amphibian's impressive bulk. Making great use of the pole's natural flexibility, he fired the salamander into the distance, where it disappeared into the vastly sparse, spade-like leaves of the undergrowth.

"I was just thinking," answered the boy.

"Of what?" asked the infant.

"Of Christmas," he announced. "The Christmas of the fairy-tale scourges. I mean, was that me, or some kind of false memory?"

Intrigued, the baby turned her full attention to the conversation, orbs and harbingers forgotten.

"Tell, tell," she requested.

"You *know* that story," sad the boy, lamenting.

"I do," said the baby. "But I shouldn't tire of it."

Tilting his head, he peered theatrically into his apparent past.

Yuletide, some years ago. The boy sits among others of similar age, comfortable and content. The air is heavy with the aromas of seasonal food and aromatic spice. The light is dim, pleasant, reflected upon the extravagant decorations. On the television set people are foolish, lewd; indicative of the children's temporary amnesty from adult supervision. Innocence, with a smear.

The boy was happily occupied, playing with a computerised video game, killing and plundering in glorious jolting neon while the others jostled and argued amongst themselves. Soon, the parents would return. Times like these were few and precious, and often the strongest, most enduring memories are borne of rare times.

The boy heard the front door opening in the hallway, but paid it little heed, assuming, quite rationally, that it was the adults returning from the bar circuit. Even as it became apparent that the noises from the hallway were a trifle aggressive to be caused by *the adults*, a child's blind faith kept him engrossed in his video game. The adjoining door was rudely bulldozed open without the benefit of the handle, tearing away part of the door frame and sending a shower of splinters floating in the scented air. In the remaining aperture stood a monstrous beast, taller than a man, and twice as broad. Its eyes, tiny and feral, spanned an enormous nose, like the bridge of a boot, and textured as such. The great nose floated atop an equally prodigious mouth, like a loamy hole in which to plant a tree. The boy sat frozen with fear, and watched in disbelief as the troll (for he knew it was so) marched across to the thrall of shocked children and seized the nearest by the ankles. As if it were an habitual and customary normalcy, the invading troll hoisted the infant high and lowered its fearful, struggling form into the maw of his mouth like the baby-eating demon of Bern.

Our boy, stricken with terror, fixated on the television set, perhaps hoping that the world inside the tube, and all its stark, blissful indifference would eradicate this most urgent and perverse predicament. The program appeared to be as utterly ridiculous as the situation in hand. It featured a man attempting to hail a taxi (a most dated, classic vintage), whilst harbouring a kitten inside his shirt and a grasshopper in his left fist. To compound his frustrations, it was raining heavily, and the animals' welfare were of vital importance. The kitten, in its distress, clawed repeatedly at the flesh of the man's torso; adversely, his resulting anxieties threatened to crush the delicate body of the tickling grasshopper. Both had been a somewhat bogus gift from the man's childhood friend Booter Bennet, a man in the grip of melancholy, facing imminent departure from the town of his youth.

Averting his gaze from the forlorn television set, the boy realised that all but himself had hence been swallowed by the rampaging troll. His friends were gone, and the brutish creature was furtling for further bullion, tearing at the plush cushions of the settee. Its attention elsewhere, the boy simply crept to the front door, dropped his melodic video game in the garden, and made off into the night.

"Gott sei dank!" the infant exclaimed. "Whatever happened next?"

"I ran," said the boy. "And I kept on running, across streets and gardens. There was nobody around."

"And what of the beastly child-swallowing troll?"

"I never saw it again. But then there was a witch, on a broomstick." He paused, thoughtful. "Are you *using* me right now?" he asked of the baby.

"No," she assured. "Tell me of the witch."

He continued, under duress.

The boy fled from the breached house, his slippered feet slapping on the flagstones, then softly bumping over lawns, the two-tone rope from his gown flying behind him in the severe December wind. He reached the outskirts of the housing estate and ran into the surrounding fields, practically oblivious to the cold, and heedless of the scratching, clutching hedgerows. As he ran, the terrain began to steepen, and he gradually became aware of a further presence behind him, a presence of evil among the rushing of wind through a million tails of tattered fabric. He turned to see the witch, a token, pantomime witch with green skin, a hooked, warty nose and clad in a dense and endlessly shredded garment, undulating like a black seaweed and similarly harbouring unknown, unspeakable threat within its dark folds. He ran on, his legs turning to jelly as he ascended, his lungs seared by the cold air, yet still he dared not stop. Reaching a summit, he faced a chilling quandary.

"Pray, whatever did you do?" demanded the baby.

"I jumped," he answered. "And kind of glided down to the foot of the heap with my dressing gown. There were policemen everywhere, so naturally, I thought I was safe."

"You glided?" queried the baby. "Not glid?"

"I glided, I think. That's 'ardly the point. The witch caught up with me, and destroyed the entire police force. She just blew them up. Then I was bitten by a bloody big snake with tin teeth. I can't remember anything after that."

"You really are the most out*rage*ous liar!" she exclaimed. "Witches, trolls and snakes! How positively trite!"

The boy slumped upon a mossy mound. "Well, it *feels* like it really 'appened."

He stared into the distance, into the far-reaching foliage through which he'd propelled the salamander. He imagined the great and powerful 'morph as a soft doll, helpless and plush, and with a miniature hand-held television set in place of her head. Flicking with exaggerated force, he randomly navigated the push-button channels, interrupting the transmission of the baby's pathetic, diminished cries, and creating horizontal scrolling lines of interference across the green liquid crystal display of her face. For a time he relished the helplessness of her flaccid limbs, and the relative silence from her gummy, pixelated mouth.

"There's a letter for you," the infant interrupted. "From a Keith and Heather."

The boy turned sharply, his curiosity piqued as to how correspondence should manifest in this jungle-zone they currently occupied. Where the infant had been seated, an unfamiliar friend stood, evidently awaiting a response.

"Where are we?" our boy asked, not wishing to appear at all unsettled or discombobulated.

"Waiting for Keith and Heather," his friend grumbled robotically.

Looking around at what was, a moment ago, green and lush, the boy observed a typical landscape of half-remembered dreams; the house that we all return to in the inescapable throes of nightmares, the containment of myriad mysteries. The room in which they stood was prodigious and carpeted, save for a border of premium standard wood flooring that shone brilliantly; at least until you looked *properly,* until you truly *saw* the colours. The carpet itself was period patterned and largely blood-red, equally extravagant, unless you noticed the balding, and the dust and the arrangements of tiny bones. At first glance (which was all that was expected of the gullible), one could easily have overlooked the wear and tear, the pigeon droppings, the smell of foist and the grime covered windows, fringed with ropes of tattered draperies, and whose meagre light complimented the dour mood of the building and all of its sinister secrets. Around the waiting pair were many tables, polished and equidistant, unpatroned and spare.

"Well, hello," enthused a forceful, feminine voice from behind the pair of circumstantial friends.

They turned, and were greeted by their hosts, the sickly-sinister sycophantic Keith and Heather. Heather, far from the soft and floral suggestion of her name, had the darting, aggressive eyes of a hungry chicken, the beak-like, Jewish nose to match, and a quickly apparent, overbearing manner that verged on unpleasant. Keith simply stood, contentedly and confidently, as if basking in the glory of his empire of illusion, his farcical fortification of falsehood.

The boy and his assumed companion were given a perfunctory introduction to the great house, that is to say, something of a plastic welcome. They were led on a rather basic tour, encompassing their lodgings and part of the grounds. Along the way, the boy observed several unsettling things, including partially shrouded security cameras, patches of dried blood that shimmered in and out of his field of perception like a grisly heat-haze, and a poignant, recurring vision of a seated room partially flooded with water. The black, filthy liquid reached the top of the chair legs, and radiated an aura of lethal danger, suggesting the concealment of an unspeakably foul and unseen portent. Continuing the facade of the grateful guest, our boy behaved as naturally as he could muster, until being released into the relative privacy of their digs. He sat on his assigned cot, watching his strange room-mate unpack his tiny collection of undoubtedly vital kit.

"What's going on here?" he enquired of the odd fellow.

"L'Andross," the young man introduced himself. "There's always a way out," he added, mechanically, accompanied by a measure of erratic twitching.

“What does that mean?” the boy asked, and was ignored.

In the cool stillness of night, in the ambient dark, our boy stretched out with his senses and detected little. On his tongue remained a flavour of the meal he'd been served in the great kitchen, a repast unfamiliar to his tastes; somewhat bitter, and reminiscent of nervous times spent overseas. He saw shadows, delightfully still, and heard only the rhythmic respiration of the bizarre machine-boy with whom he shared the near silence. He smelled only dust, and felt only the slightest of draughts skating across the contours of his exposed skin. Sleep, he decided, was ill-advised, and restful sleep was fantasy. He rose, hurriedly dressed himself, and with a cursory glance at L'Andross, padded barefoot from the dimness of the sleep chamber. Somewhat unsurprisingly, the hall by which he'd entered it, differed from the hall into which he exited. He walked as quietly as he was able, enticed by a flickering light that revealed itself to be a wall-mounted video console periodically displaying various sections of the house. Although poorly rendered, the objectives of what he saw were obvious, but the impetus was unclear. Among the selective panoramas were armed guards.

Armed guards stood by cars; armed guards with masks, at large.

Dogs patrolled, the beasts were smart.

Strangers ran from those in charge, beaten, shot and torn apart.

The boy was in trouble; imperilled, thou art.

“I can't escape,” he thought. “I can't.”

He ran to the end of the hall, to a door which, upon inspection, was unlocked and led to the house grounds. Galvanised by the sudden and rhythmic clicking of dog claws upon wood flooring behind him, he stepped outside and closed the door, satisfied at the sound of its lock engaging between himself and the approaching canine. Soft, cool rain fell upon his face, inducing a comforting sense of deja-vu. He surveyed his surroundings and found himself to be in a kind of quadrangle, with the main building at its centre, surrounded by a high wall topped with barbed wire. The extensive tangles of barbed wire had taken many trophies, it seemed. Forever ensnared within its knots and loops were litter, indistinct tatters of fabric, animals in varying stages of putrefaction, and even human skeletons, twisted and exposed amid their eternal ballad. A great swathe of tarpaulin had been snagged at the corner junction of what he hoped was the perimeter wall, and in this he pinned his hope of escape. Voices, urgent and cold, alerted him to his compromise, and he ran.

In the heat of the moment, in the desperation of tantalising notions of freedom, his reality began to *twist.* Everything slowed. The raindrops burst upon his face with such exaggerated, balletic labour, the cries of his pursuers elongated and deepened. His joints seemed to stiffen, as if fusing into one comprehensive bone. Gravity appeared to increase, turning every movement into an intense, and seemingly puerile effort.

Despite these compounded hardships, he reached the corner, and leapt at the tarpaulin, clutching desperately. To his astonishment, it held as he hefted himself up to hopeful freedom. In places it tore, as did the rusted barbs upon his flesh, but still it served until he was able to drag himself, bleeding, up upon the parapet. Gathering the tatters of the tarpaulin behind him, lest he be pursued, the futility of his situation fell upon him like the increasingly heavy rain. He hadn't time to clamber over the mesh of barbed wire; he'd be shot, even if he avoided disembowelling himself within its razor tangle. The guards readied their guns, the sound of cocking piercing the tranquillity with impossible, laboured clarity. Ahead of them bounded a gigantic black dog, sweating and steaming about the flank. Visibly, the boy submitted to fate, and readied himself for death. Closing the distance quickly, the dog scaled the wall with supernatural ease, and approached our boy until its sour, misty breath fell upon him, much as his hopelessness had done.

His eyes tightly closed, he waited, Seconds ticked by like minutes, but expiration didn't manifest. Opening his eyes but a sliver, he saw that the dog was seated before him, its tongue and flews undergoing a strange, almost alien sequence of motions. It began to articulate, at first conveying only a yawning sound, then, as if learning anew, it began to sing.

"Yesterday's flowers may be dead, but a black rose blooms in the well of my soul. And its thorns will draw blood."

The dog, it seemed, had no desire to kill him.

"He only wanted to sing," said the boy, only partially relieved.

ACT 5 – My Mare

Dark were the streets at night, and dangerous, but delicate Dan walked them anyway. All around him, as far as the eye could see (or the mind imagine) lay dirt. His stout, practical shoes collected dirt as he walked, and were partially rinsed by lesser concentrations of dirt, a suspension of undrinkable water in the puddles along the kerbs. The streets were filth, the houses dank, with pipes piping water that nobody drank. Clothes and bedding hung forgotten from sagging washing lines, caked with grime; the washing machines themselves long dormant, idle. He dug his hands deeper into the pockets of his hooded coat, trying to stymie the cold wind that so consistently distributed the litter about the damaged suburb of My-Mare, and chilled the stones of the broken homes.

Dan felt vulnerable as he walked, to the elements, to the pervasive violence of My-Mare, and to a dozen other influences he either hadn't considered yet, or wasn't able. He viewed the tragic landscape through the aperture of his zipped hood, favouring the ill-conceived comfort of narrowing his field of vision, and therefore resultantly narrowing potential threat to himself (the ostrich theory). His quick, awkward gait spoke of his displeasure at having to venture beyond his comfort zone. Focussed on his limited horizon, he pressed on.

Traders lay ahead. Traders ran bars; traders *in* bars traded unfavourably from cars. The few establishments Dan was familiar with were situated beyond the tortured landscape of a small, hilly playground he'd frequented as a child. Long gone were the carefree days of assembling dens among the prickly, berry-laden bushes and trees, although even then it seemed every adventure was tainted by some subtle and sour flavour of the future. The crackling blue lights of Harper's Bazaar reflected upon the wet roads ahead. Dan favoured Harper's above the others, a favouritism borne of familiarity. He liked the heavy, metallic clang of the bell which alerted Harper to another potential transaction, and the unique, indiscernible aroma that would outlive Dan, Harper and generations of future patrons, blissfully aloof.

A voice from behind him waylaid everything.

"Hey," said a male voice. "I can do you some business."

Approaching footsteps accompanied the voice, and delicate Dan tried to suppress the too-familiar feelings of panic. He quickened his pace as subtly as he could muster, staring longingly at the relative safety of Harper's Bazaar and the indistinguishable shadowy figures he could see through the windows. In his own mind, he had become as prey, his soft, white underbelly metaphorically exposed to predators and scavengers alike.

"Hey, I know you," the voice went on, and a hand grasped loosely at his sleeve, rasping sharply against the tight weave of the fabtric, then letting go.

Tardily, and rather too enthusiastically, Dan snatched himself away from his perceived aggressor and faltered.

"I can do you some business."

In his alarm, Dan thought, particularly vividly, of unkempt dwellings; ancient, frayed and balding carpet, spotted with fallen plaster congealed to paste by irascible damp. He thought of bare pipes, their surfaces corroded, spent and useless, visible within crumbling walls with thin, timber laths exposed like thrashed ribs. Wind whistled through the shattered windows in his mind, the cracks and fissures too narrow to permit escape for the starving, forsaken pets that dragged themselves hopelessly along on fragile, failing limbs. Pitiable, disease-pocked bones were their destiny, with no-one to spare the pity. Pitiable bones grown old alone. Damp bones in hell, laid low and too weak to moan. Fur-speckled bones, honed of flesh and blown dry like stone.

"I know you. I can do you business."

-O-

Safe as could be in his lofty keep, *the boy* tentatively raised his makeshift periscope to the window of the tower. Only one unbroken pane remained in its semicircle frame; one of seven. In its glory days, the window had consisted of six wedge shapes and one smaller semicircle at the centre, proud and gleaming. Today, as the boy and the petulant baby sheltered within, it resembled a ravaged gum, although still quite beautiful in a most enigmatic, Gothic fashion. His periscope reeked, constructed from mirrored tesserae mounted within the stiffened pelt of a hollowed cat. Spotted and scratched, the tiny tiles nevertheless performed their integral function quite admirably. The long-suffering boy surveyed a scene.

-O-

Below the tower, a great garden was dotted with partygoers, gambolling amid much frivolousness. In one direction, houses stretched off into the distance, and in the other direction the garden gave way to a great moor. Already darkening, Mare Moor exuded a powerful sense of foreboding that, it seemed, only Chris “the cat” could detect. He dismissed this unwelcome discomfort as a side-effect of the alcohol and drugs that had rampaged through his system for the better part of a week, and tried to enjoy this remaining time away from his scholastic program. These days of celebration had been great; a total lapse from any kind of responsibility, be it social, moral or *other*. The garden fire had blazed for days, rekindled each morning. From its zenith, sparks flew, twisting into the blackening sky and fading, only to be replaced by more, so long as the flames were fed. So long as the heart of the inferno bled red, the shadows fled, holding nary a stead.

Chris returned his attention to his friends; the first love, you lose. You choose in twos.

“*Let's do the moors!*” someone yelled, and free from democracy, free from collative organisation, they fled shrieking into the wilds, disappearing quickly.

“Hey,” said Chris. “That's not such a good idea. There's, like, five hundred square miles of wilderness.”

His concerns went unheeded, and his friends voices diminished as the the shadows deepened. Only one girl remained. She approached the fire and sat.

“You're not joining them?” he asked.

“Just looking for adders in the dark, Marcus,” she answered. “Shake, Marcus. Shake.”

Puzzled, he joined her at the fireside and they chatted, the conversation wide-ranging and unrestrained.

After a time, Chris became aware of the chill of night, and the amalgamation of the shadows into complete dark.

"Hey, they've been gone a long time."

The girl's attention was lost among the twirling flames, floating easily atop the white heat of the tortured embers. Chris tried to listen beyond the crackling of the burning wood and discerned nothing, until a distant scream, bereft of any trappings of joy tore through the night air like an explosion. The scream held no fear and no hint of pain, nor did it trouble to ring out again. The scream was hate.

Flinging his drink in a reflex action, Chris jumped to his feet. He looked over to whence the scream had come.

"What the *FUCK* is that?" he whined, his voice strangled by fear.

From the inky blackness of the moors a hag had come, and he knew it was so, because what else could adopt a form that perverted the laws of nature to such a vile extent? Smiling a smile set too wide, the creature advanced on the remaining party of two, surrounded by a glow of origin unknown. Her thin arms outstretched, they extended far beyond human capabilities, and were a marriage of human and vegetation, the cool night breeze whistling through flesh, leaf and tendril as they swung above her head. Scuttling on the legs of a bat, she continued toward them.

Chris watched the gap closing between himself and this Lovecraftian monstrosity, noticing also that similar glows were becoming visible in the distance. It dawned upon him with horror that these wisps were his companions, doubtlessly malformed and changed as was the hag, and hope began to fail him. He could not combat what had returned from the moors. What of his friends, and this hag to be shorn, as she tore through the corn adorned with bramble thorns? He turned and fled blindly. Forsaking the too-temporary amnesty of the house, he scrambled frantically up onto the garage, then began to clamber up to the roof, his fingers bleeding in their passion for survival. Grasping and scraping, he found enough purchase to reach the chimney, to which he clung like the cat of his namesake. Perfectly still and silent, he sat, his arms around the column of bricks, hopeful of concealment within the shroud of night. Within moments of his hopeful seclusion, invasive and alarming, something cold and moist alighted upon his trembling hand. Looking down, he saw a black, newt-like creature crawling confidently, purposefully across his fingers, its wet, glistening head shaped like that of a baby bird. Splitting the eyeless appendage in two, its wide jaws opened and clamped upon one of his fingers; the pain was sudden, and impossibly intense. Recognising the newt as a facet of the hag, he relinquished his grip on the chimney and flung the tiny creature towards the fire, which now ate hungrily of the girl with whom he'd talked earlier. More of his luminescent former friends assembled and watched, unrepentant of what their collective had done. Others joined the hag in her former guise, assembling cannons pointed at the house upon which Chris “the cat” sat, and that was that.

-O-

The boy lowered his periscope and withdrew from the window.

"Oh, how does it look?" asked the baby, stretching dramatically, as if roused from slumber.

"Brown," the boy answered. "Code brown."

"What on earth does that mean?" she asked.

"I'm not sure. It just seemed appropriate," he answered, morosely. "Everything is brown."

The baby sighed gently. "You know, sometimes you really are the most crashing bore."

"What would you rather I told you?" he asked. "The truth? There's more sprites coming out of Mare Moor!"

"What are they, theses *sprites*?" asked the baby, intrigued. "Animals? Monkeys, spiders and little pygmies?"

"I saw a witch, and some kind of elf."

"That's new," she said, thoughtfully. "No wolf this time?"

"No," he answered. "Not yet."

"Look forth to My-Mare," the baby instructed.

Reluctantly, the boy resumed his position at the window and raised the stinking periscope again.

-O-

Far from the moors, in a field, in a tent, two lovers embraced passionately. Rain drummed in a deluge upon the tiny textile erection, creating a most ambient and memorable atmosphere, enhanced by the glow of the streetlights on the splashing water as it blew ghost-like along the deserted streets. The entrance to the tent was open, its curled flaps beating against themselves in the wind. Their intimacy displayed to all, adding spice to their ardour. Timothy sat cross-legged on the ground sheet, his lady straddled across him, facing him, his swollen manhood deep within her slippery fold. Raindrops warmed as they drew myriad courses down the skin of her back, chilling her as they stole precious heat.

“Close the tent. Please?” she requested.

“It's a bit late for that,” Tim answered. He reached behind her, regardless, and anxiously drew the three sets of zips together, meeting them in the centre. The noise of the storm abated, somewhat, and their lovemaking resumed in earnest. Breathlessly, they chased their mutual conclusions. Clawing and moaning softly, they held each other tightly on the desperate brink. What to think, arriving in sync? Take a moment to blink before you sink, because eventually we *all* sink. Moments later, they were lashed by the rain again, this time from all directions.

“What the hell?” she exclaimed.

Looking around them, the tent had disappeared. It hadn't been uprooted or blown away, it had simply gone. As they surveyed their immediate surroundings with increasing alarm, they noticed that the closest houses had also vanished, leaving only barren soil, quickly becoming mud.

“Aliens?” suggested Tim, nervously.

"Your mother," the girl answered, and began collecting her damp clothes, which, to her gratitude, although strewn, remained untampered.

Tim followed her lead. He drew his cold, uncomfortable garments about himself, wincing at their sodden touch like that was the greatest of their current concerns.

"What now?" he asked of her.

"Jesus, let's just go," she answered, and made off, scampering in the direction of the town of My-Mare.

The rain continued to assault them in their departure, seeming to spin around them in miniature vortices of cold and annoyance. Their hair adhered to their heads, and their sodden clothes rubbed irritatingly against their pink, sensitised skin. Drainpipes sluiced their excessive cargo into the streets, creating sparkling streams as the full moon adorned the many tributaries with diamonds.

From the direction of town came the sound of multiple footsteps, rhythmic and regular.

"Hey, who's that?" cried the girl.

"Hello. Can you help us?" Timothy shouted, cupping a hand over his eyes to see better through the elemental onslaught.

Approaching them from the gloomy streets ahead there appeared three military figures, their badges suggesting law-enforcement. In procession, they jogged close to the buildings. To their breast, each held a baton, and each wore a shining silver helmet, a flawless and glistening silver dome with visors shielding their faces from the rain, and somewhat obscuring their identities. The figure at the rear wore a communication radio at his hip. The radio crackled with static and stuttering fragments of conversation from atop the starched piping of his trousers. The three men seemed as indifferent to the attempted transmissions as they were to the two soaking wet individuals hailing them from the road.

"Hey, can you hear us!" shrieked the girl.

"*Hey, Chips*!" shouted Tim, disgruntled at their ignorance.

Realising that the three men intended to pass by in a state of nescience, Timothy stepped forward in anger, shoving the rear guard a touch more firmly than he'd intended. The man struck the wall hard, his pristine headgear creating sparks as it bit momentarily into the brickwork. He collapsed onto the wet pavement, his radio detaching from his belt and spinning to a halt, still issuing its tinny dialogue.

"An ex-employee even claims to have played it," the radio barked as it gathered raindrops.

The remaining two military figures jogged nonchalantly into the dark distance as their fallen colleague lay motionless.

"The juvenile dog has a flick-knife," the radio went on. "Not hostile, but cautious."

The accumulated water put paid to further transmission, as the radio popped and fell silent.

-O-

Delicate Dan, the most unfortunate man, described a meandering track of deep, waterlogged footprints along the muddy shore of My-Cove. The dark, fetid sands sucked at his bare feet and ankles, longing to sink him into the depths of the mire and hold him in eventual death like a forgotten secret. Each time he fell, he clawed at the gritty compound, heedless of the increasing wealth of galling particles beneath his fingernails. Every time he struggled back to his feet he ploughed onward, aimlessly purposeful. The khaki sands caked his body, adding mass to his plight. Beneath his vacant eyes, tears had drawn twin tracks of purity upon his cheeks. This was hope, and hope was fading biologically.

Dan seized a long, flat rock with bleeding, swollen fingers, and heaved its considerable mass into a standing position. He scoured the uncovered area with his eyes, seeking his elusive salvation among the darkest recesses of the shores. Another pocket of nothing had lain beneath the rock, only shining bubbles and more brine. Leaning back carefully, lest the sucking sands trip him, he released it. Amid a fine and far-reaching scattering of grain and moisture, the barnacle-encrusted slab fell with a resounding and satisfying slap upon the wet sand, which, despite his dour misery, Dan relished. Undaunted, he extended his trail of desolation, and moved on to another stone.

Some diners watched the lamentable spectacle of delicate Dan with vague interest from a nearby restaurant window. Advertising a sea view, the business held good to its promise, with a bonus of this forlorn cabaret. An oriental gentleman regarded the hapless act with great scrutiny, his fat throat jiggling as he shook his head almost imperceptibly in bewilderment, nevertheless peering consistently from behind inconceivably thick, round spectacles.

Unaware of the performance he was providing, with flesh rent aplenty, and sand and stone colliding, Dan strove on. His strength waning, his mad eyes were filled with fear; yet seeing no sense in complaining that hope was not here, he moved forward inexorably.

Raising another stone, a rivulet of blood oozed from beneath one fingernail, falling into the pattern of a bone-white v-shaped scar adorning the skin between the knuckles of his right index finger, and turning it red.

-O-

"What of Sarah and the round rooms?" asked the baby.

"It's still showing," the boy answered, referring to the television show being broadcast from a retrospectively collectible television set in the restaurant outside which Dan was failing.

"Well, what's happening?" she asked.

"The house is full of geese," said the boy. "And some bees."

"Then what of My-Mall?" she demanded.

Turning the cat-periscope in his hands, he regarded its stricken countenance. The creature looked, unsurprisingly, resentful of its fate, its teeth bared in anger. Its dried, blackened eyes had long ago receded into their sockets, all hope rescinded. Around its neck hung an identity collar, the strap discoloured from unpleasant seepages. The identity tag said LUCKY. What greater irony, unless the tag had read PURITY?

-O-

The great, resplendent wood-panelled walls of My-Mall stretched off above the heads of the gaggle of teenagers until their edges blurred, such was their grandeur. The young adults drifted into the mighty precinct in such stereotypical teenage-pulp-fiction form that their individual identities were of no import; their singularities so indistinct that their characters were unworthy of the lavishness of depth and texture within this narrative, save for two. Young Stamper hung close to the exquisitely pretty girl Eloise, his affections noted (and obvious), but not yet reciprocated. The cluster of youth edged its way into the throat of My-Mall, divided among its split levels, enraptured by its vast emptiness, and its long amnesty from the human touch.

The huge vertical expanses of stained timber were decorated with a variety of truck relevant to an obsolete culture. Great glass cases displayed portrayals of movie characters long forgotten, heroes for an allotted time only. Podiums held statues, although mass-produced, well-loved within their limited microcosm.

Eloise and Stamper paused beneath a poster depicting a cartoon dinosaur of historically accurate proportions, its paper trim stained with the ochre of age. The dippy-looking creature beheld a mask of confusion, skilfully artistically compounded by its exaggerated underbite and a whimsical wig that would have poorly complimented any given period. The prehistoric animal was coloured a perfect, clean magenta.

"Who is that?" asked Eloise.

To Stamper, her question was like an excerpt from a song, almost whistling from her sweet throat, and falling upon his ears like a fine rain, warm, fragrant and soothing. "I have no idea," he answered.

Eloise moved along dismissively, graceful and elegant. Stamper soon followed, pulled by the invisible force that he was too young to fully comprehend, and powerless to defy. They rejoined the others, kicking their careless way through ages of dead leaves and twigs that diminished as they approached the dark belly of Mr-Mare. Another picture had attracted the group's attention. This one, far from being a mass-produced film advertisement, was a textured piece of abstract art, simultaneously unique and worthless. White, puckered lines divided the blotched and pebbled canvas skin, mottled to a colour similar to bruising. Such was the terrain that the equidistant lines threw fascinating shadows across the troubled landscape. Recognising the linear legend before him, Stamper gazed down at the scarring on the back of his hand, the origin of which seemed indistinct, like a half-remembered dream. It was a perfect match for the series of right-angled slashes before him on the wall, the incomplete squares displayed beneath the glass.

Catching his distraction, Eloise reached out and took his hand, at once appreciating the uncanny similarity. "Wow," she murmured.

Drawing a thumb slowly across the scar, feeling its irregularity, Eloise unwittingly sent a powerful rush on a journey, climbing Stamper's arm from the wrist in a twisting, tickling, ever-increasing surge, finally culminating in his brain with a sensation graphically akin to the sudden ascent of a great flock of birds.

Such was the feeling, that Stamper was momentarily intoxicated, the aftershock crawled teasingly across his scalp like pins and needles before disappearing altogether. His head reeling, he returned to the reality of the dusty old shopping mall. Eloise tugged lightly at his hand, and made off into the shadows with the rest of the group.

"Come on," she enthused, smiling.

Turning, he looked back at the square of light from whence they'd come; explorers and scavengers, thrill-seekers, leaders and followers alike. What prizes held yesterday? What guises and deceptions were underway? Surmises in all shapes and sizes, curiosity's reprises. *Oh, please, won't you stay? It's like forever when you've goned away.*

He bounded after them, dashes of fading colour amongst the creeping, leaping shadows.

"Hey!" hissed Eloise, appearing from behind a waist-high barrier. She leaned tantalisingly forward, gripping the dulled brass rail that ran along the barrier's edge. To Stamper, nothing had ever looked more beautiful, more entirely perfect, and nothing would again.

Galvanised, he moved toward her, and leaned in to kiss her sculpted lips. At the last moment, she giggled softly, teasingly, and moved fluidly away, reminiscent of a dolphin. Carried by momentum and the clumsiness that often accompanies innocent love, he followed through with the kiss and for a brief, immaculate moment, his lips lightly brushed the milk-white skin of her chest as she swerved.

An explosion of white light before his eyes, images and emotion in his mind; the soft smoothness of a partially-inflated balloon, the pliant, forgiving, unbroken surface of cool water, and old boxing announcer captured on flickering, jolting black and white film, striking the bell and declaring “That's a *knockout!*”

Stamper was lifted off his feet as if skewered, his arms raised at his sides like Christ. He sailed backwards through the air in slow motion, gracefully enraptured. Executing a perfect arc, his body eventually came to a halt among the dust and leaves, landing softly like a falling feather. On his back among the debris, he stared at the barely discernible ceiling, and for a time, everything was correct. This was a *new* thing, and things are only new once. *One night only, tomorrow I'll be gone*. This was purity, before the innocent are tarnished by years and experience. This was a pearl, a diamond, a baby's breath. This was a moment, like the instant of death; singular, isolated. For this slice of now, Stamper was a smitten romancer. Prone in the dark, he knew love is the answer.

“Love *is* the answer.”

-O-

“You saw all this?!” the baby asked.

“What else is there to see? I believe I've seen everything.” He dropped the cat-periscope.

“Don't be so utterly melodramatic,” she admonished.

The boy's head hung low, heavy. “What difference can one man possibly make?”

"History is filled with single men who made a difference."

"Yeah, they're called martyrs, and among the primary essential requirements of being a martyr is the stipulation that you're fucking dead!"

The baby sighed, a far-off look in her eyes. "I'll tell you of martyrs," she said. "One day."

17626756R00032

Printed in Great Britain
by Amazon